"Are you sure you want a h[...]
mum asked her. "You would [...]
kitten or a puppy? It's your b[...]
can have which you like."

"I'd like a hamster and a kitten *and* a
puppy," said Rosie. "And a rabbit and a gerbil
and a goldfish and a horse and an elephant.
I'd like lots of animals."

"Dad said just one," said Rosie's mum.

So Rosie chose me.

When Bumble the hamster gets chosen as
Rosie's pet, he knows he's got an important
job to do. Discover how hard he has to work
in this delightful, funny Young Corgi story –
ideal for building reading confidence.

www.kidsatrandomhouse.co.uk

YOUNG CORGI BOOKS

Young Corgi books are perfect when you are looking for great books to read on your own. They are full of exciting stories and entertaining pictures. There are funny books, scary books, spine-tingling stories and mysterious ones. Whatever your interests you'll find something in Young Corgi to suit you, from ponies to football, from families and friends to ghosts. The books are written by some of the most famous and popular of today's children's authors, and by some of the best new talents, too.

Whether you read one chapter a night, or devour the whole book in one sitting, you'll love Young Corgi books. The more you read, the more you'll want to read!

Other Young Corgi books to get your teeth into:
BLACK QUEEN by Michael Morpurgo
LIZZIE ZIPMOUTH by Jacqueline Wilson
SAMMY'S SUPER SEASON by Lindsay Camp
ANIMAL CRACKERS by Narinder Dhami

BUMBLE

*With thanks to the
boy who gave me the idea*

BUMBLE
A YOUNG CORGI BOOK : 9780552558990

PRINTING HISTORY
Young Corgi edition published 2001

Set in 17/21pt Bembo

Young Corgi Books are published by Random House Children's Books,
61–63 Uxbridge Road, London W5 5SA,
A Random House Group Company

Addresses for companies within The Random House Group Limited
can be found at: www.randomhouse.co.uk/offices.htm

THE RANDOM HOUSE GROUP Limited Reg. No. 954009
www.**kids**at**randomhouse**.co.uk

A CIP catalogue record for this book is available from the British Library.

Printed and bound in Great Britain by
Cox & Wyman Ltd, Reading, Berkshire

Bumble

Alison Prince

Illustrated by Doffy Weir

YOUNG CORGI

Chapter One

Rosie came into the pet shop and
saw me at once.

"Oh, Mum, isn't he sweet!" she said.
"Look at his pink nose and his little
paws!"

I was only three weeks old at the
time, so I suppose I was quite sweet.

"Are you sure you want a hamster?"
Rosie's mum asked her. "You wouldn't
rather have a kitten or a puppy? It's
your birthday – you can have which
you like."

8

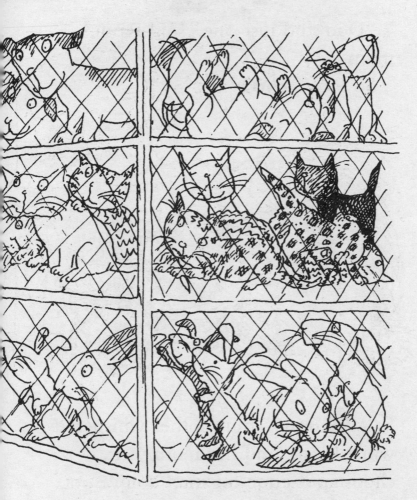

"I'd like a hamster and a kitten
and a puppy," said Rosie. "And a
rabbit and a gerbil and a goldfish and
a horse and an elephant. I'd like lots
of animals."

"Dad said just one," said Rosie's mum.

So Rosie chose me.

"Well done," my mother whispered while Rosie and her mum were choosing a cage for me. "You've got the job. Remember, it's up to you to keep your people happy. Goodbye, dear, and good luck."

I felt very special, getting a job like that at only three weeks old.

"Dad, look!" said Rosie, when we got home with me in my new cage. "Isn't he sweet?"

"He's got a big bum," said her dad. "We could call him Bumble."

So they did. I thought it was a bit rude. I mean, humans have big hands and feet, but I wouldn't call one of them Handle or Footle because of that. But I didn't complain. It was my job to keep my people happy, so I got on with it.

I did Running Up the Sleeve and
Pocket Diving and Washing My Face
on Rosie's Shoulder. They all liked
that one.

Then I went on to Ear Tickling and Hair Climbing, which made them squeak a bit. The things they liked best were Finger Balancing and Hanging From the Pencil.

I was a bit scared they'd drop me, but I had to be brave. All part of the job.

The next evening, I did it all again, and added a bit of Trouser Exploring and Trainer Nibbling (never again — it tasted horrible).

When I was in my cage, I watched carefully to see what sort of games my people played among themselves, in case I could join in later. Their favourite seemed to be Hide and Seek. They were always rushing

about, shouting, "Where are my car keys?" or "Anyone seen my glasses?" or "I can't find my socks!" Then they'd find the thing they'd lost, and they'd look pleased and say, "Thank goodness!"

So that evening, I hid myself under the sofa and thought they'd enjoy finding me.

Wrong.

They started shrieking and shifting the furniture about as if I'd gone for ever. I thought I was going to get squashed, so I hid

under the TV, but they moved
that as well. I ran up a table leg
and found myself on a big thing
with square buttons that went up
and down under my feet, and
Rosie's dad shouted, "Get off my
computer!"

Hide and Seek was a terrible failure,
so I sat very still and let Rosie catch
me and put me back in my cage.

She was very nice about it, and
gave me a seed bar that was so big
I couldn't get it into my food store.
They all laughed at that, but I felt
dreadful. It was my job to keep them
happy and I'd made my first big
mistake.

When Rosie and her mum and dad had gone to bed, I ate most of my seed bar and thought seriously about my job. Tomorrow, I wouldn't play Hide and Seek. Definitely not. I'd have to find something to put in its place, though. Maybe I could try some Lampshade Balancing.

But I didn't get the chance. When Rosie's dad came home from work the next day, he brought a see-through plastic ball made of two halves. They put me in it and joined the halves, then put the ball with me inside it on the floor. I could trundle about, rather like running in a wheel, but the ball was too big to go under the sofa.

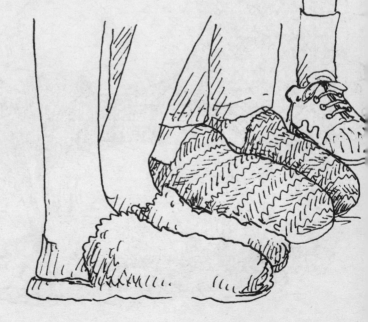

There was no way I could play
Hide and Seek, even if I'd wanted to.
Rosie and her mum and dad thought
it was great fun, watching me motor-
ing around in my see-through ball,
but I wasn't so sure. I couldn't do
Chair Climbing or any kind of
Exploring the Surroundings. After a
while, I began to get a bit bored.

Rosie still did some Handling and Carrying when she felt like it, but sometimes she was busy with other things, and I had to stay in my cage.

I spent a lot of time moving my food stores about. Rosie gave me heaps of delicious things to eat –

she was great about that. Nuts and
seeds, bits of carrot and apple and
celery, sometimes a strawberry or a
segment of orange, leaves of dandelion,
grass – there was no end to it.

There was more than I could eat by
a long way, but I enjoyed organising
it. And of course, I ate as much as I
could. I didn't want to seem ungrate-
ful. I started to get rather fat. Not just
my bum, but all over. I needed more
to do, and I did wish I could get out
and explore.

Chapter Two

One night, just as I'd turned everything out of my food store to
rearrange it, I saw two mice. They
had their skinny little hands on the
bars of my cage, and they were
staring in.

"Wow," said one of them. "What
are you going to do with all that
food?"

I didn't answer. My mother had told me never to speak to mice. "They're not like us," she had said. "They have no cheek–pouches, poor things, so they can't carry things about. They're hopelessly untidy. Not like us at all."

"Come on, Fatty," said the mouse. "Give us a sunflower seed, I'm hungry."

"Me, too," said the other one.

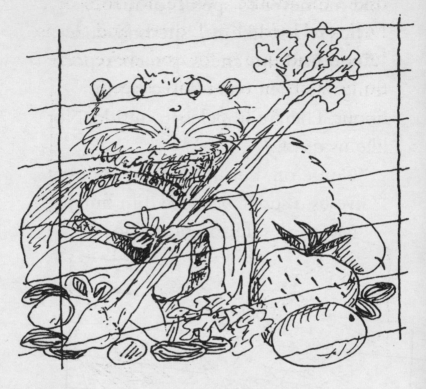

"My name is not Fatty," I said, "it's Bumble. And this food belongs to Rosie and her family. They give it to me because I keep them happy, but I can't go handing it out to every Tom, Dick and Harry – it's more than my job's worth."

"What's Tom got to do with it?"
asked the mouse. "We're not Tom or
Dick or Harry, I'm Darren and this is
Janice. And you're fat and we're thin.
So how about a sunflower seed?"

"Oh, all right," I said. "Just one."
And that's where I made my second
big mistake.

★

The next night, Darren and Janice came back with two friends.

"Hallo, Bum," said Darren. "This is Kevin, and that's Marlene. Where's the sunflower seeds?"

"Sorry," I said firmly. "No sunflower seeds." This time, I'd made sure everything was hidden away, out of sight.

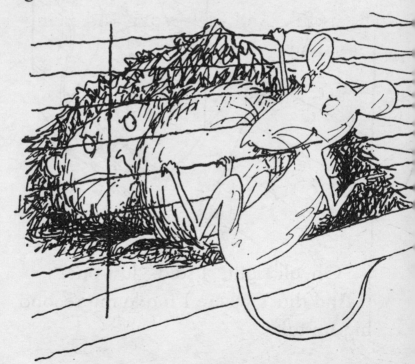

"Who are you kidding?" said Darren. His nose was twitching. "You've got lots of sunflower seeds in there, I can smell them. Peanuts, too."

"Find your own food," I said crossly. "You're out there, free to run around, you can find what you want. I'm stuck here in my cage."

"Poor Bumble," said Janice. "It must be awful." And I felt really bad, being pitied by a mouse.

Kevin ran up the side of the arm-chair and said, "Hey, look! Crisps!"

"Those are Rosie's," I said. "Leave them alone."

But they didn't, of course. They tore the packet open and scattered bits of crisp all over the place, nibbling here and there, picking pieces up and dropping them. I saw exactly what my mother meant, they really were hopelessly untidy.

"These Ready Salted make you thirsty, don't they?" said Marlene. "Anyone coming for a drink?"

"Good idea," said Darren. And off they all went, leaving the floor covered with crumbs and torn bits of packet.

I felt terrible. I should never have spoken to them, let alone handed out a sunflower seed. It was all my fault – and Rosie's mum and dad were not going to be happy at all.

Chapter Three

"We've had mice!" said Rosie's mum the next morning. "Oh, my goodness, what a mess!"

"Mice are sweet," said Rosie, but her dad disagreed.

"Mice are a pest," he said. "They'll have to go. I'll ring up Mr Cook next door. He's a practical man – drives the Council dustcart. He'll know what to do."

★

Mr Cook came round that evening, when Rosie had gone to bed. He brought mouse traps and put them in lots of places on the floor, each one with a lump of cheese on it. "One nibble and they're dead," he said. "Bingo."

I was glad Rosie was in bed. She wouldn't have liked this idea at all. I didn't like it myself, to tell the truth. Darren and Janice and Kevin and Marlene were untidy, but I didn't want to see them turned into Dead Bingo, whatever that meant.

When the mice came that night, I said, "Be careful! A man came and put traps down with cheese in them, but one nibble and you're Dead Bingo."

"No problem," said Darren. "My grandad showed me what to do with traps. Watch this."

He stood to the side of one of the traps, and poked it.

WHAP!

The spring came down so hard that I jumped, even though I was safe in my cage.

"Now you can eat the cheese," said
Darren, "but don't touch the others
till I've dealt with them, OK?"

"OK," said Janice, Kevin and
Marlene.

By morning, the four of them had
eaten all the cheese and went burping
off home, leaving the carpet covered
with crumbs.

★

"Oh, ho," said Mr Cook the next day. "Clever mice we got here." He gave me a nasty look. "That hamster is your trouble," he said. "Once you got one of them in the house, it attracts the mice. You best get rid of it."

"Oh, no!" said Rosie. "We can't get rid of Bumble! He's my pet and I love him, he's sweet!"

"Sweet it may be, but you want to get rid of it all the same," said Mr Cook. "Clear the mice out, then you can start again. Stick insects are nice."

"I don't want a stick insect," said Rosie. "I want Bumble."

"Maybe we could get a cat," said her mum. "That would keep the mice away, wouldn't it?"

"Worth a try," agreed Rosie's dad. And Rosie thought a cat would be sweet.

So off they went to see Mrs Cats-Home.

Chapter Four

Rosie and her parents came back with Augustus. He was huge and lazy, with big feet and long grey fur. "A cushion," he said. "Oh, how nice." And he lay down on it and went to sleep.

Rosie's dad looked at him and said, "I think we've made a mistake."

"He's sweet," said Rosie. "He's got lovely golden eyes."

"But they're always shut," said her dad.

"That's because he's just eaten a whole tin of cat food," said Rosie's mum, "and drunk half a pint of milk. He's resting."

But Augustus rested all the time.
When the mice came that night, he
opened half a golden eye, then shut it
again. After what Mr Cook had said,
I was worried. What if I got sent back
to the pet shop? I couldn't face telling
my mother I'd lost my job because of
encouraging the mice.

Darren and the others were
giggling at the sight of Augustus.
"Call that a cat!" said Kevin.

"More like an old hearth rug," Marlene agreed.

"Got long whiskers, hasn't he?" said Janice.

Darren said, "Bet I can grab one."

He crept up the cushion and tugged at a whisker – and Augustus sneezed so hard that he blew Darren across the carpet.

Then he rubbed his nose with a fat, grey paw and murmured, "Please don't do that." And went to sleep again.

"Boring," said Marlene. "What are we going to eat? There's no mouse traps tonight. No cheese. Give us a peanut, Bum?"

"Certainly not," I said. "Find your own." Then I wished I hadn't, because they said, "OK," and trooped off into the kitchen. I could hear paper being torn and stuff spilling about, and merry squeaks from the mice.

"What's this white stuff?"

"Sugar. Mm, nice!"

"Oh, look, cornflakes!"

"Hey, look, if you bite a hole in the packet, all the stuff comes running out!"

"Brilliant! Let's have a go."

Shut in my cage, there was nothing I could do about it.

"Augustus!" I hissed. "Wake up!"

Augustus yawned and said, "Why?"

"You've got to do something about the mice," I told him. "They're in the kitchen, mucking things up. Go and frighten them."

Augustus yawned again. "Can't," he said.

"But why not?" I was getting frantic. "Don't you catch things? Can't you at least *pretend*?"

"No," said Augustus. "I caught a beetle once, because it fell on me. I let it go, though."

"But—" I began. It was no use. Augustus had gone back to sleep.

In the morning, Rosie's mum and
dad were frantic, too.

"Just *look* at this kitchen!" said Rosie's
mum. "What on earth am I to do?"

"I'll get Mr Cook," said Rosie's dad.

★

"Only one thing to do," said Mr Cook. "Get rid of the hamster and the cat, put down poison. Now, that stuff *really* works. Smells lovely, but just one taste and – bingo."

"But we *can't* get rid of Bumble and Augustus!" wailed Rosie. "I love them, and they're sweet."

"So they may be," said Mr Cook. "But there's no other way you'll get rid of the mice."

"We could try a dog," said Rosie's mum. "Couldn't we? Mrs Cats-Home has dogs as well."

"All right," said Rosie's dad wearily. "But this had better work, because the whole thing is driving me insane."

Chapter Five

Rosie and her parents came back
with Geraldine. She was white, with
long legs and black eyes and a black
nose, and she was woolly all over,
specially on top of her head.

"Isn't she sweet!" said Rosie.
But her mum and dad didn't
answer.

That night, Geraldine was so scared of the mice that she jumped on the table and stood there, shaking all over.

"They're going to run up my legs!" she said. "I know they are. They'll nibble my wool and nest in my ears, I can't bear it, I think I'm going to faint."
The mice fell about laughing. They left Geraldine shaking on the table and went into the kitchen for their supper. Then they came back, wiping their whiskers and ready for a game.

"Call that a dog?" said Darren. "More like a sheep on stilts, isn't it!"

He and Kevin ran up the table leg, and Geraldine gave a shriek of terror and jumped off. The mice chased her round the chairs and over the rubber plant, across the sofa and behind the TV, then out the other side. In her panic, Geraldine accidentally trod

on Augustus, who woke up and
thought *he* was being chased, so both
of them went rushing round the room
with the mice after them. I never
thought Augustus could move so fast.
He and Geraldine both leapt onto
Rosie's dad's desk and ran across his
computer.

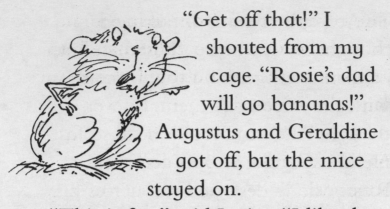

"Get off that!" I shouted from my cage. "Rosie's dad will go bananas!" Augustus and Geraldine got off, but the mice stayed on.

"This is fun," said Janice. "I like the way these little buttons go up and down. And what's this mat with a clicky thing on it? Just the right size for us!"

"It's a mouse mat," I told her – then wished I hadn't.

"Oh, great!" said Marlene.

"You can slide on it, look. The clicky thing's a sort of car!"

The computer started making funny pictures because one of the mice had jumped on the ON button. I closed my eyes in horror.

As I'd expected, Rosie's dad went bananas.
"Just look at this!" he roared.

"Who's been mucking about with my computer?"
"Not me," said Rosie and her mum together. They looked very tired, because there had been a lot more chasing last night, and a lot more noise.

Augustus and Geraldine were totally wrecked. I was all right, because I'm always up at night, but I was worried sick about what was going to happen.

"That's *it*," said Rosie's dad. "I've had enough. The dog and cat are useless, so they can go back where they came from and so can the hamster. I'll phone Mr Cook."

"But you *can't*!" shrieked Rosie. "I love Bumble and Augustus and Geraldine, they're  *sweet*! Oh, Dad, *please*!"

Rosie's dad was still bananas.

"Then *you* do something about it," he said. "Because I'm at my wits' end. I'm off to work. Goodbye."

And he stumped out without any
breakfast.

"Oh, dear," said Rosie's mum.
"What are we to do?"

"I'll fix it," said Rosie. "The animals
just need to understand, that's all.
Leave it to me, I'll talk to them."

"Best of luck," her mum said, and
went off to the kitchen to see if the
mice had left anything to eat.

Rosie shut the door and said,
"Now, listen, all of you. Augustus,
wake up, this is important. And
Geraldine, stop shivering, you're just
being silly.

"You really do have to get rid of the mice. I know they're sweet, and I know you've been trying hard, I could hear you chasing them about all night. But it's not good enough."

Augustus and Geraldine looked at each other guiltily. Rosie didn't know it was the mice who'd been chasing them.

"You have to be *really frightening*," said Rosie. "Because otherwise, you'll be sent back to Mrs Cats-Home and Bumble to the pet shop, and Mr Cook will come, and . . ." Her eyes filled with tears.

Chapter Six

"I'd like to help," said Geraldine when Rosie had gone to school. "I really would. But it's my nerves, you see. I'm so scared."

"And I'm so tired," said Augustus. "I'd like to help, I really would. But every time I see one of these nice, soft cushions, I just . . ." And he was asleep again.

All right for some, I thought.

I hardly slept all day for worrying.
At last I decided that Rosie had the
right idea. But it wasn't us who had
to understand, it was the mice. And it
wasn't Rosie who would talk to them.
It was me.

When I woke up at
tea time, Rosie was
saying to her dad,
"It'll be all right. I've
told the animals
what to do, and
the mice won't
come any more.
You'll see."

"Well, it's their last chance," said her dad. "Any mouse trouble tonight, and it's Mr Cook and the you-know-what." And he unplugged the computer, just in case.

When Rosie and her mum and dad had gone to bed, the mice came chattering in, as cheerful as ever.

"What, no new animals?" said Kevin, looking round. "Shame. That was getting to be fun."

"Listen," I said. "LISTEN! This is important."

They laughed, but they came and sat outside my cage.

"Go on, then, Bum," said Darren. "What's so important?"

"If you go on mucking about," I told them, "Mr Cook is going to put down poison. It'll smell lovely, but just one taste and – bingo."

The mice looked gloomy.

"What a downer," said Marlene. "Just when we'd found a nice place."

"Funny lot, humans," said Darren. "Not exactly friendly, are they?"

"But look," I said. "You've really upset Rosie and her mum and dad. And Mr Cook told them it's my fault for encouraging you. And—" I found this difficult to say "—I do quite like you. I'll miss you when you've gone. But I won't be here, either. They'll send me back to the pet shop, and Augustus and Geraldine back to Mrs Cats-Home. I'm sorry. I suppose I should never have given you that first sunflower seed, then this would never have started."

The mice were quiet for a moment,

then Darren said fairly, "Well, it might have started. I mean, we've got to find food somewhere, haven't we? All right for you, sitting there with more than you can eat."

"But I do get bored," I said. "I envy you sometimes, being free to run around."

"Why didn't you say?" asked Janice. "We could let you out, any time you wanted. We're good at opening things."

I stared at her. And then I had my great idea. "Why don't we do a swap?" I said. "You let me out for a run, and I'll give you the food I don't need."

"Brilliant!" said Kevin.

"BUT," I went on, "there's to be no mess. No going in the kitchen, no chasing the dog and pulling the cat's whiskers. And keep off the mouse mat, OK? Otherwise it's Mr Cook and Bingo."

"OK," said Darren.

"We'll be good," said Marlene. "Cross my heart and hope to die. Well, almost." And they all laughed.

In the morning, Rosie's dad looked round and said, "I don't believe it. Not a trace of mice anywhere. Not a crumb, not a dropping – nothing."

"Marvellous," said Rosie's mum.

And Rosie said, "Told you I'd fix it."

I was back in my cage with the door shut. Darren and Janice and Kevin and Marlene had tidied up all my stale bits of apple and old peanuts.

"They just needed to understand, you see," said Rosie, pouring milk on her cornflakes. "Things will be fine now."

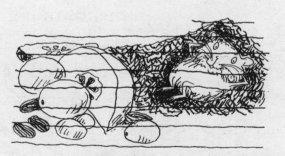

And they were. I didn't mind Rosie thinking she'd fixed it – anything to keep my humans happy.

I was happy, too, running about at night with my friends, the mice. And Mrs Cats-Home gave Rosie a new friend, too – a rabbit. She calls him Bingo. I don't know why – but that's humans for you. Very sweet, but no sense really. They'd be lost without a good hamster to look after them. Rosie's all right though – she's got me.

THE END